DANNY AND THE EASTER EGG

by Edith Kunhardt

 Greenwillow Books, New York

Magic Markers and a black pen were used
for the full color art.
The text type is Avant Garde Gothic Book.
Copyright © 1989 by Edith Kunhardt
All rights reserved. No part of this book
may be reproduced or utilized in any form
or by any means, electronic or mechanical,
including photocopying, recording or by
any information storage and retrieval
system, without permission in writing
from the Publisher, Greenwillow Books,
a division of William Morrow & Company, Inc.,
105 Madison Avenue, New York, N.Y. 10016.
Printed in Hong Kong by South China Printing Co.
First Edition
10 9 8 7 6 5 4 3 2 1

Library of Congress Cataloging-in-Publication Data

Kunhardt, Edith.
Danny and the Easter egg.
Summary: Danny colors Easter eggs with
his friends, then hunts for them after
they are hidden by the Easter Bunny, and
gives a special one to his grandmother.
[1. Easter eggs—Fiction.
2. Easter—Fiction]   I. Title.
PZ7.K94905Dal 1989   [E]   88-1164
ISBN 0-688-08035-9
ISBN 0-688-08036-7 (lib. bdg.)

To my sister Nan
and our special Easter memories

Danny and his friends are
coloring Easter eggs
with dye and stickers
from a special kit.

They dip their eggs into
the dye. Then they let them
dry on the table.

Lucy's favorite egg is striped.

"Yum. It's almost like candy," she says.

Mark's favorite egg has spots.

"This is for my Mom," he says.

Joshua's favorite egg has stars
on it. "Like the sky," he says.

Danny draws a D for Danny on an egg.

He dips the egg into the color.

The D comes out white.

The egg comes out red.

"This is my Danny egg!" he exclaims.

Danny waves good-bye to his friends.
"Happy Easter," he calls. His friends
take their eggs with them.

After dinner it is time for bed.
Danny puts his eggs into his Easter
basket. He leaves the basket at
the bottom of the stairs.
"I hope the Easter bunny hides these,"
he says.

"Good night, Danny," says
his father. "Happy Easter."
"Good night, Danny," says
his mother. "The sooner you go
to sleep, the sooner you will wake up."

When Danny wakes up in
the morning, the sun is shining.
He looks out the window.

Danny runs downstairs.

He sees his empty basket.

"The Easter bunny came!" he yells.

He grabs the basket and

runs out into the yard.

Danny begins to search for eggs.
First he looks up in a tree.

There is no egg in the tree, but
Danny finds one under a bush.
"My blue egg!" he cries.
He puts it into his basket.

Danny looks for another Easter egg.

He looks behind a stone.

There is no egg behind the stone,
but Danny finds some jelly beans and
a chocolate bunny in the tall grass.
He puts them into his basket.

Danny goes on looking.

He looks in the flower bed.

There is no egg in the flower bed.

It is on the fence.

"My Danny egg!" Danny cries.

He puts it into his basket.

Then Danny sees something amazing.
He sees a coat hanging from a tree.
It is a beautiful new coat with shiny
buttons. "That is your new Easter
coat, Danny," says his mother.

"Try it on," says Danny's father.

So Danny puts on the coat.

"It fits! I love it!" he cries.

He does a little dance.

"Now let's visit Granny," says Danny's
mother. She puts on her Easter
hat. Danny's father puts his Easter
flower in his buttonhole.

"Don't you look nice!" says Granny.

"I have a present for you, Granny,"
says Danny.

He gives her his Danny egg.

"Thank you, Danny! Happy Easter,"
says Granny. And she gives him
a big Easter hug.